A NOTE TO PARENTS

Reading Aloud with Your Child
Research shows that reading books aloud is the single most valuable support parents can provide in helping children learn to read.
- Be a ham! The more enthusiasm you display, the more your child will enjoy the book.
- Run your finger underneath the words as you read to signal that the print carries the story.
- Leave time for examining the illustrations more closely; encourage your child to find things in the pictures.
- Invite your youngster to join in whenever there's a repeated phrase in the text.
- Link up events in the book with similar events in your child's life.
- If your child asks a question, stop and answer it. The book can be a means to learning more about your child's thoughts.

Listening to Your Child Read Aloud
The support of your attention and praise is absolutely crucial to your child's continuing efforts to learn to read.
- If your child is learning to read and asks for a word, give it immediately so that the meaning of the story is not interrupted. DO NOT ask your child to sound out the word.
- On the other hand, if your child initiates the act of sounding out, don't intervene.
- If your child is reading along and makes what is called a miscue, listen for the sense of the miscue. If the word "road" is substituted for the word "street," for instance, no meaning is lost. Don't stop the reading for a correction.
- If the miscue makes no sense (for example, "horse" for "house"), ask your child to reread the sentence because you're not sure you understand what's just been read.
- Above all else, enjoy your child's growing command of print and make sure you give lots of praise. *You are your child's first teacher — and the most important one. Praise from you is critical for further risk-taking and learning.*

— Priscilla Lynch
Ph.D., New York University
Educational Consultant

For Morgan, my muse
And in memory of Dolly, her pony
— Love, Lucy

Library of Congress Cataloging-in-Publication Data

Alistir, K. A.
    My ponies / by K.A. Alistir ; illustrated by Lucinda McQueen.
       p.   cm. — (Hello reader! Level 2))
    Summary: A girl imagines the many wonderful ponies she will have when she grows up and thinks about how she will enjoy their company.
    ISBN 0-590-25489-8
    [1. Ponies — Fiction. 2. Imagination — Fiction. 3. Stories in rhyme.]
  I. McQueen, Lucinda, ill. II. Title. III. Series.
PZ7.A3984My 1996
[E] — dc20   95-13238
                                              CIP
                                              AC

12 11 10 9 8 7 6 5 4 3 2 1   5 6 7 8 9/9 0/0

Printed in the U.S.A.   23

First Scholastic printing, December 1995

My Ponies

by K. A. Alistir
Illustrated by Lucinda McQueen

Hello Reader! — Level 2

SCHOLASTIC INC.
Cartwheel B·O·O·K·S·®
New York Toronto London Auckland Sydney

When I grow up
I know what I'll be.

A keeper of ponies.
Just wait and see.

I'll have brown, white, and black
ponies—

short ones and tall.

All ponies are welcome.
Come one! Come all!

We will live on a farm
in a big purple house.

I'll have chickens
and cows,

a dog
and a mouse.

We will all eat pink cupcakes
and drink strawberry milk.

I'll brush pony hair
till it's soft as fine silk.

My ponies will run.

My ponies will roam.

Then they'll come back
to our home sweet home.

When my ponies get tired,
I'll tuck them in beds.

We will all go to sleep
with sweet dreams in our heads.